A Shape Scavenger Hunt

by Kerry Dinmont

The Child's World®
childsworld.com

Published by The Child's World®
1980 Lookout Drive • Mankato, MN 56003-1705
800-599-READ • www.childsworld.com

Photographs ©: De Visu/Shutterstock Images, cover (top left), 3 (top left), 5; Mindscape Studio/Shutterstock Images, cover (top middle), 3 (top middle), 19 (bottom left); Rob Hyrons/Shutterstock Images, cover (top right), 3 (top right); Maryna Pleshkun/Shutterstock Images, cover (bottom left), 3 (bottom left); Shutterstock Images, cover (bottom middle), cover (bottom right), 3 (bottom middle), 3 (bottom right), 7, 11, 12, 13 (top right), 13 (bottom right), 17 (left); iStockphoto, 4, 6, 9 (top left), 9 (bottom), 14, 16, 19 (top), 20, 21; Supanee Sukanakintr/Shutterstock Images, 8; Frank Romeo/Shutterstock Images, 9 (top right); Giorgio Magini/iStockphoto, 10; T. T. Studio/Shutterstock Images, 13 (top left); Konstantin Yolshin/Shutterstock Images, 13 (bottom left); Tanya Rozhnovskaya/Shutterstock Images, 15; Maya Kovacheva/iStockphoto, 17 (right); Anthony J. Hall/iStockphoto, 18; Roman Samokhin/Shutterstock Images, 19 (bottom right)

Design Elements ©: Maryna Pleshkun/Shutterstock Images; Mindscape Studio/Shutterstock Images; De Visu/Shutterstock Images; Rob Hyrons/Shutterstock Images; Shutterstock Images

ISBN 9781503823662
LCCN 2017944883

Printed in the United States of America
PA02361

About the Author

Kerry Dinmont is a children's book author who enjoys art and nature. She lives in Montana with her two Norwegian elkhounds.

Shapes are everywhere. Everything around us has a shape. Turn the page to see if you can find the different shapes in this book!

Some shapes have straight sides. Triangles have three straight sides. All sides may be the same length. Or the sides may be different lengths. Some road signs are shaped like triangles.

How many triangles are on these sailboats?

5

Squares have four sides. Each side is the same length.
Rectangles have four sides, too. Rectangles have two
short sides and two long sides. The opposite sides of
a rectangle are the same length.

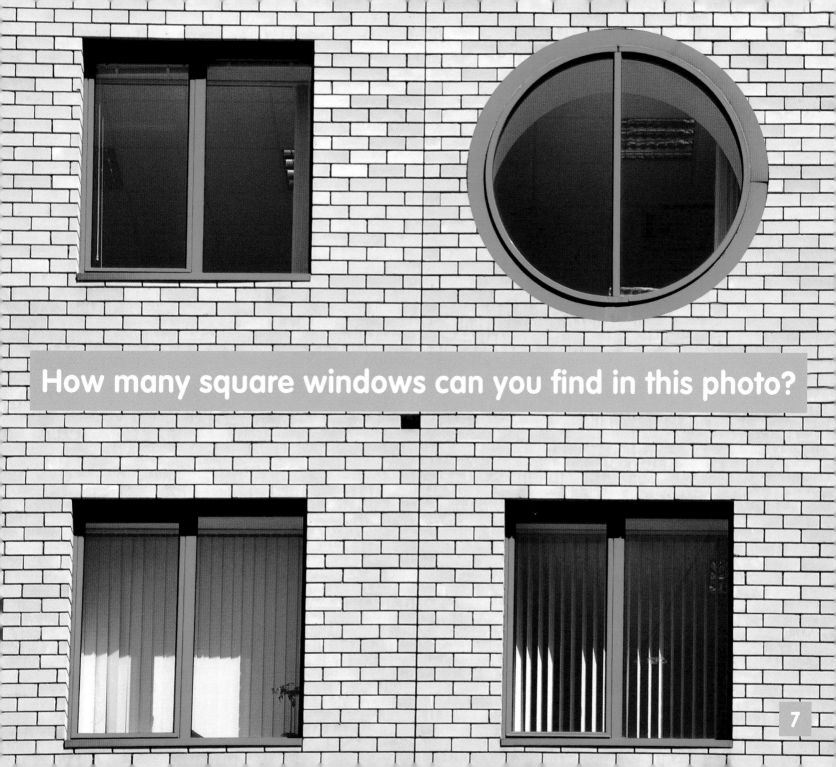

How many square windows can you find in this photo?

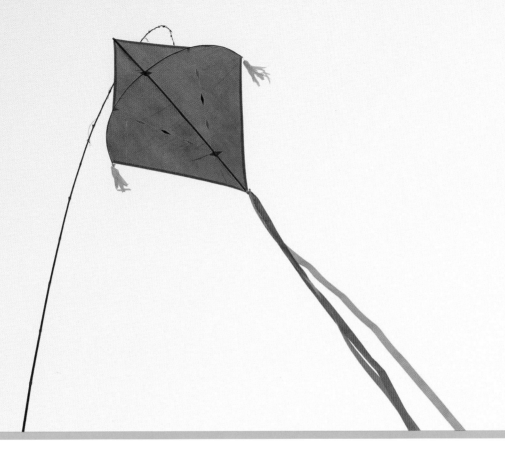

Diamonds also have four sides. Their sides are the same length. Diamonds are like squares that lean or slant to one side. Two triangles can make a diamond. Kites are often shaped like diamonds.

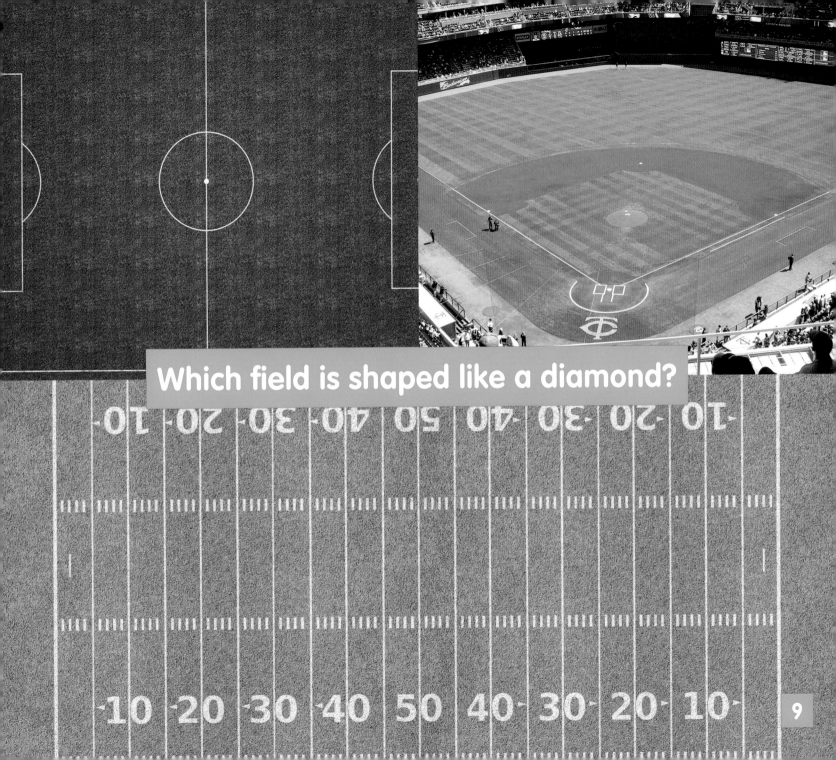

Which field is shaped like a diamond?

Some shapes have many sides. Octagons have eight sides. Each side is the same length.

A star is another common shape. Stars have five or more points.

Which of these flags have stars?

13

Some shapes are round. A circle is made of one line that **curves** around. All points on the line are the same distance from the center of the circle. Ovals are also round. They are like **squashed** circles.

Can you find the circles in this parking lot?

Hearts also have two sides. If you draw a line down the center, the two **halves** are like a **mirror image**. Each half starts at the top of the line. It curves up and away from the line. Then it comes back down toward the line. It meets the other side at a point at the bottom.

Which candy is shaped like a heart?

A crescent has two sides. Both sides are curved. A crescent looks like a sliver of a circle. Sometimes the moon is shaped like a crescent.

Which food is shaped like a crescent?

The world around us is made of shapes. There are many kinds of shapes.

What shapes do you see in this kitchen?

Answer Key

Page 5   **How many triangles are on these sailboats?** There are four triangles on these sailboats.

Page 7   **How many square windows can you find in this photo?** There are three square windows in this photo.

Page 9   **Which field is shaped like a diamond?** The baseball field is shaped like a diamond.

Page 11   **Can you find the octagon in this photo?** The stop sign is shaped like an octagon.

Page 13   **Which of these flags have stars?** The two flags on the left have stars.

Page 15   **Can you find the circles in this parking lot?** The car tires are shaped like circles.

Page 17   **Which candy is shaped like a heart?** The red lollipop is shaped like a heart.

Page 19   **Which food is shaped like a crescent?** The croissant is shaped like a crescent.

Glossary

curves (KURVZ) Something that curves bends in a line that is not straight. A circle is made of one line that curves around.

halves (HAVZ) Halves are two equal parts that can be combined to make a whole. You can see the two halves of a heart when you draw a line down the middle of the shape.

mirror image (MEER-ur IM-ij) A mirror image occurs when one half of an object or a drawing is the same as the other half, but reversed. The two halves of a heart are like a mirror image.

opposite (AHP-uh-sit) Something that is opposite is across from, or facing, something else. The opposite sides of a rectangle are the same length.

sliver (SLIV-ur) A sliver is a very thin, pointed piece of something. A crescent shape looks like a sliver of a circle.

squashed (SKWAHSHD) Something that is squashed is flattened or crushed. Ovals are shaped like squashed circles.

To Learn More

Books

Alexander, Emmett. *Sort It by Shape*. New York, NY: Gareth Stevens, 2016.

Pistoia, Sara. *Shapes*. Mankato, MN: The Child's World, 2014.

Walter, Jackie. *What Shape Is It?* London, England: Franklin Watts, 2016.

Web Sites

Visit our Web site for links about shapes:
childsworld.com/links

Note to Parents, Teachers, and Librarians: We routinely verify our Web links to make sure
they are safe and active sites. So encourage your readers to check them out!